HOW TO EAT PIZZA

Cooked up by head
chef and dish washer
Jon Burgerman

SLICES

Jon Burgerman's favourite kind of pizza is a simple cheese and tomato Margherita, with added garlic and basil. A basic cheese slice is the true test of a good pizzeria. He also likes eating one slice of red pizza (that has no cheese on it) and then one slice of white pizza (that is tomato-less). Jon did not truly appreciate the magical qualities of pizza until he moved to live in New York, where there is a lot of good pizza. Jon enjoys all kinds of pizza, even including 'dollar slices' and the impossible to eat with your hand Chicago deep pan variety.

SALADS

Pizza is perfectly accompanied with salad. Jon really likes salad too, especially colourful ones with lots of nice ingredients like peppers, alfafa sprouts, cucumbers, olives, nuts, beets, avocado, pickles, a sliced boiled egg and spinach. Make friends with a salad, you won't regret it!

WE DELIVER
sometimes

OXFORD
UNIVERSITY PRESS

Great Clarendon Street, Oxford OX2 6DP

Oxford University Press is a department of the University of Oxford. It furthers the University's objective of excellence in research, scholarship, and education by publishing worldwide. Oxford is a registered trade mark of Oxford University Press in the UK and in certain other countries

Text and Illustrations © Jon Burgerman 2018

The moral rights of the author and illustrator have been asserted
Database right Oxford University Press (maker)

First published 2018

British Library Cataloguing in Publication Data

Data available

ISBN: 978-01-9-274952-9

10 9 8 7 6 5 4 3 2 1

Main text set in Burgerman 1.7 with the permission of the author

Printed in China

Paper used in the production of this book is a natural, recyclable product made from wood grown in sustainable forests. The manufacturing process conforms to the environmental regulations of the country of origin.

EXTRAS

This book is dedicated to Vinnie's, Fornino, Carmine's, Carmine 2's, Sal's, Tony's, Paulie Gee's, Best Pizza, Two Bros, Motorino and Emmy Squared.

Pizza and salad recipies, facts, doodles and related fun can be found at:

www.howtoeatpizza.com

Drawing of chef Jon by Madeline Babuka Black

HOW TO EAT PIZZA

Jon Burgerman

OXFORD
UNIVERSITY PRESS

How do you eat pizza?
What, you don't know?

Oh, come on,
it's really easy!

The first thing you
need to do is choose a slice.

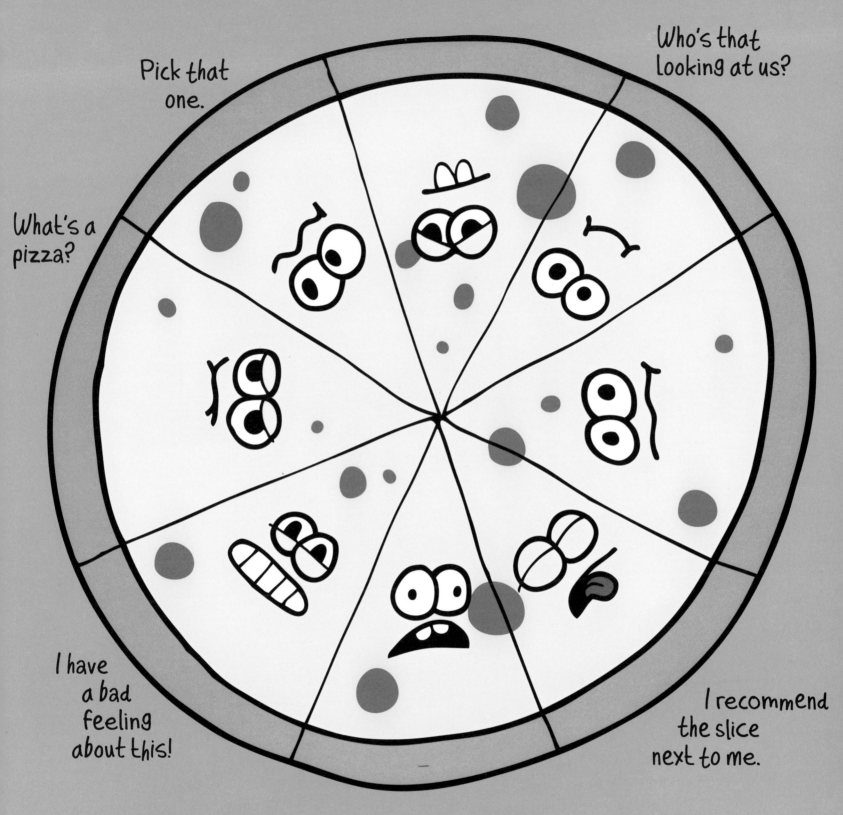

Which do you like best?

I always pick the

BIGGEST!

Aaaaaghh!

Once the slice cools down, I add a light sprinkle of chilli flakes.

And maybe a sprig of basil.

Some people like to use
a knife and fork . . .

But I don't. I like to use my . . .

'You know I have a crusty bottom, right?

No one likes the crust!'

'Slice 1 knows karate.

Slice 2 is good at computers.

Slice 3 is very musical.

$\left(\frac{b}{2}\right)^2 + h^2 = a^2$

$h = \dfrac{\sqrt{4a^2 - b^2}}{2}$

a a

Slice 4 is a perfect isosceles.

Slice 5 used to be a bank robber.

Slice 6 is a book worm

and slice 7 is a ...

'Now, hold on a minute here!
You're suggesting
they eat us? US?!'

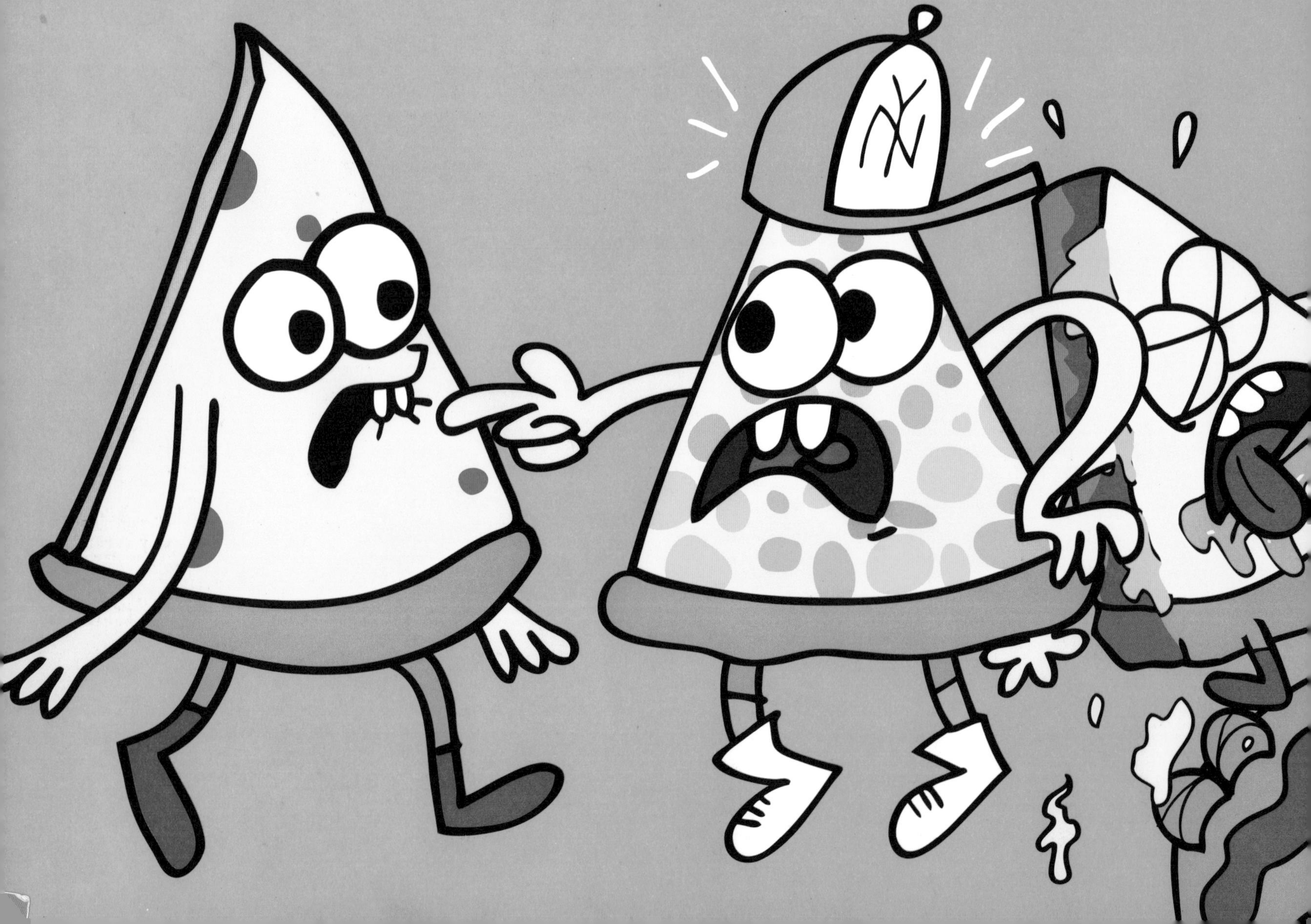

'Hey, guys, I think I've found something in this book!'

'Have they ever tried our old friends the....

... fruit and vegetables?

There's mushrooms...

Don't eat us, we're fungus!

Waaaa!

... or broccoli.
It's like a mini tree.

Save the trees!

Trees are good

and the bees!

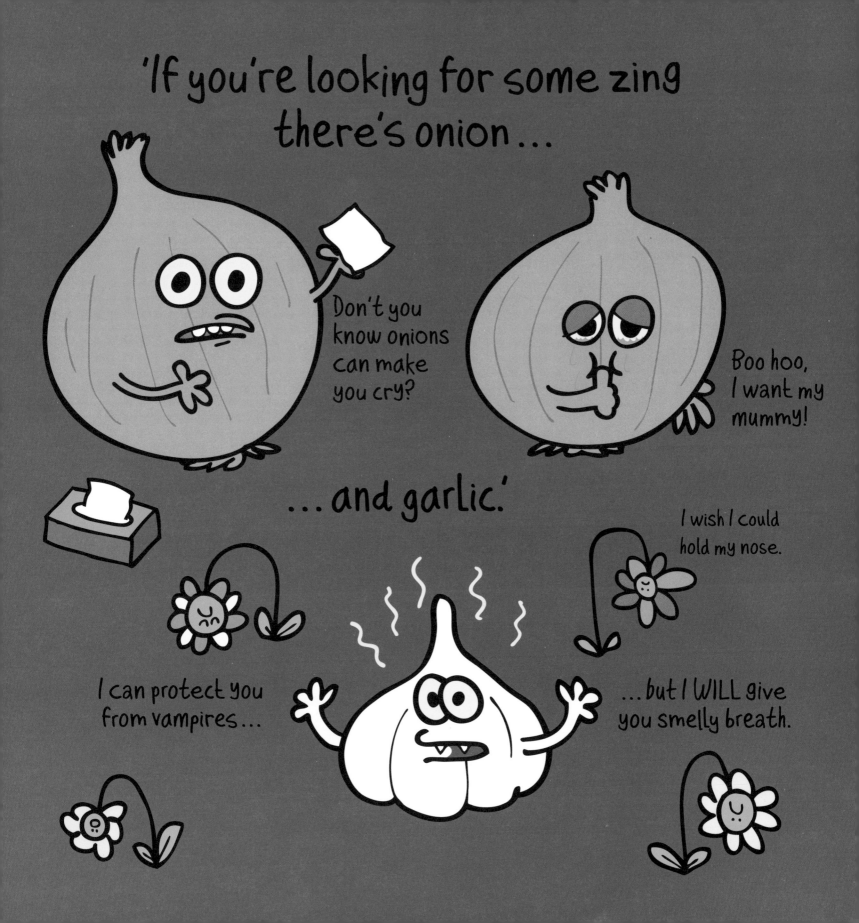

'Tomatoes are fun ...

We could splat you if we wanted.

Too late!

... and peppers are so colourful.

I may look mild but some of us pack some serious...

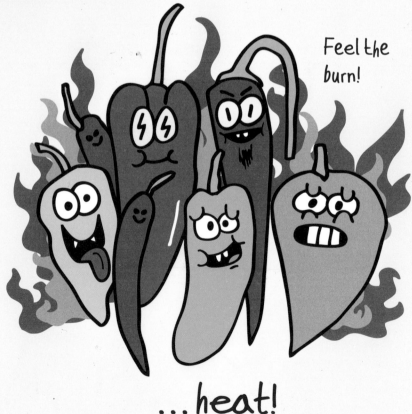

Feel the burn!

...heat!

Okay, Pizzas,
you've changed my mind.

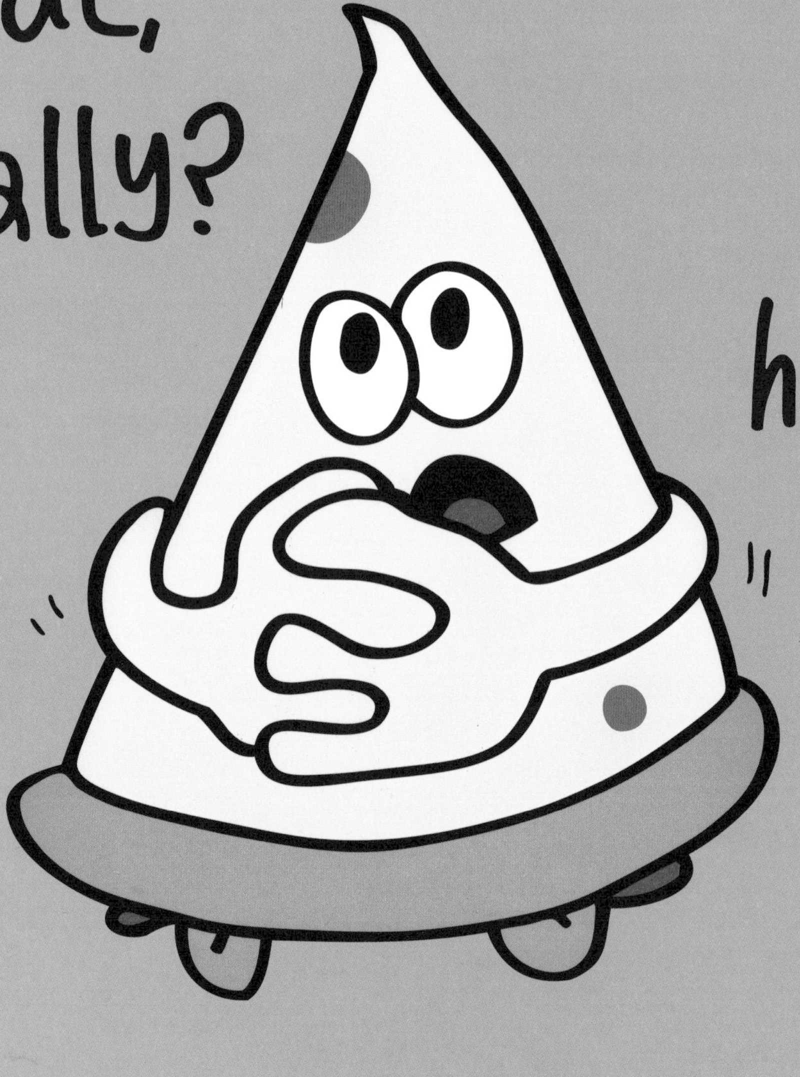

Yeah, maybe it's better to eat . . .

Now, how do you eat doughnuts?